Heartfelt Christmas

A Christmas in Baublesville

Sweet Romance

Honey Stone

Michael Villa Press

Contents

1. Chapter 1 — 1

2. Chapter 2 — 11

3. Chapter 3 — 17

4. Chapter 4 — 29

5. Chapter 5 — 43

6. Chapter 6 — 47

7. Chapter 7 — 53

8. Chapter 8 — 61

9. Chapter 9 — 65

10. About the Author & Thank You — 77

Also By — 81

Chapter 1

"Ooooh, they are soooo delicious, Liv! You've got to have them in your shop!"

"They're very expensive, Mel," Olivia muttered. "Beautiful. But too expensive for the shop, I'm afraid. We'd never be able to sell them."

"Look at the work in them, though. They're amazing. They're mouth-watering."

Olivia cast another look at the extraordinarily glorious glass work, sighed wistfully, and turned away.

Mel still drooled over the exhibition of glass Christmas baubles made by the famed recluse and master glassblower, Noah Pritchard. Out of the corner of her eye, Olivia saw Mel reach out to the biggest bauble on the display tree. The one with a sign on it saying: 'Not For Sale'.

As if she could see it happening in slow motion before it actually did, she saw her friend pick up the bauble, but it was just too big for her hand to hold securely.

It fell.

It smashed to smithereens on the floor, leaving Mel to stare at it, her lips in a round 'ooh' of surprise.

The sound of breaking glass momentarily silenced the chatter of the other visitors to the gallery.

Olivia froze in fright. It would have to be the one that wasn't for sale, wouldn't it? It couldn't have been one she could simply have paid for, so she could leave and never return to that gallery again.

Panic held her still. Noah Pritchard's prized creation was never meant to be handled, let alone destroyed by a careless member of the public.

She couldn't let herself think that if it was that prized, it shouldn't have been on show in a public place. No, she couldn't think like that. That wouldn't be right.

All she could think was – thank heaven Noah Pritchard wasn't here to see the destruction!

Olivia had to stop her friend from having some kind of horrific breakdown. Mel couldn't stop squeaking and wringing her hands. She danced on the spot and stared at the shimmery spread of tiny glass shards on the parquet floor.

Yes, Olivia knew what she had to do now – first, she'd make sure Mel was okay. Then she'd clean the place up and pay some sort of compensation to the gallery owner. Then she'd get her and Mel safely away from the scene of the crime, and home. She could relax then.

To her relief, she saw a tall figure with a dustpan and brush in his hands emerge from the back of the gallery.

He turned and called, "Rob!" over his shoulder, and waited for a second, but no one appeared.

"Thank you so much!" she cried, hurrying over to him to take the cleaning implements. "Just what I needed." She smiled up into his face. "I'm so sorry we've made a mess in your gallery. I'll just clear it up before anyone can step in it, and then you must tell me how much I need to pay you for the bauble."

She hurried back to deal with the mess of glittering fragments on the floor. Mel was still making odd noises and fidgeting, so Olivia put the dustpan down, put her arm around her friend, and led her over to a chair. She pressed her into it. "Just stay there. I won't be long. It was an accident, Mel."

Olivia hurried back and brushed up the remains of the bauble.

All the while she was conscious of the gallery owner saying nothing, just standing watching her. He made her feel nervous. She wondered if the compensation she'd have to pay was going up with every second he stared at the top of her head.

When she finished clearing up, she approached him, trying to keep her face conciliatory. "I am so very sorry for the breakage. How much do I owe you?"

She offered him the dustpan and brush. She didn't know what else to do with it.

He carefully took them off her, but he didn't answer for a long time.

Too long, Olivia thought.

Longer than necessary.

He just wanted her to squirm. And she *was* squirming, too, the longer she stood there waiting for an answer.

She wrenched her eyes away from him to search for her wallet, to find her credit card. "Here," she said, offering it to him in the continuing silence. "Please take what I owe. And while you're at it, throw in three dozen assorted baubles for my Christmas store."

Olivia just stopped herself from swearing. That hadn't been part of her plan at all! She couldn't afford all those baubles. She'd added them on because she felt so bad about the accident. Lovely though they were, those baubles would never sell in her store. They were far too expensive for 'Baubles and Bling', her shop.

But she'd said it now.

She continued holding out her card. Why didn't he take it?

Finally, she looked up to see what was taking so long, only to find grey eyes as cold as a glacier's heart regarding her as if he'd seen nothing like her before.

They made her feel exposed and awkward.

"Please," she said. "Take my card. Take the money for the broken bauble and for the three dozen."

Finally, he spoke: *"Throw in three dozen assorted baubles ..."*

"Okay. Maybe inappropriate wording for glass baubles, but you know what I mean."

"You know these baubles are all unique, don't you?" he said. "Hand made. Irreplaceable."

"I am sorry," she said. "We never meant to cause any damage."

"Maybe not, but you should have known better than to touch what wasn't yours."

Mel had appeared, her face flushed with embarrassment and regret. "I'm so sorry. I didn't mean to ruin your display. The bauble just slipped from my hands …"

But he cut her off. "Slipped from your hands? Why was it in your hands in the first place?"

Olivia had reached her limit. She hated seeing her usually bubbly friend so downcast. "Didn't it occur to you that such an irreplaceable work of art should never have been in a public space?"

"Your apologies didn't last for long, did they?"

"Repeating apologies doesn't make them more profound." Olivia knew she had what Mel called her 'pompous phone voice,' on now, but she couldn't help it. This man was making her mad. "Please. Take the money from my card so we can leave."

Finally, he took her card and went back to

the desk with it.

Mel took Olivia's arm and patted it as if soothing a snarling creature.

When he brought the card back, he said, "I've taken the money for the baubles and will have them delivered to you within the next couple of weeks. They are so specialised we don't just have them hanging around waiting to be sold." He smiled. "Or, indeed, broken."

Mel squeezed Olivia's arm hard as she felt her friend tense.

Olivia took the card and receipt from him and shoved them in her wallet. "Thank you," was all she could manage through gritted teeth.

As she turned to leave, she heard him add, "I haven't charged anything for the one you broke. It was irreplaceable and, therefore, priceless."

By the time Olivia and Mel reached the street, she was shaking with rage. He knew perfectly well that by not charging her anything for the broken bauble, she would always feel guilty about it.

"Remind me never to go back to that gallery," she said to Mel as she marched along the street. "What a stuck up, obnoxious, arrogant, supercilious, so-and-so that gallery owner is!"

They reached her car, and she hopped in. When Mel got in the passenger seat, she murmured: "That wasn't the gallery owner."

"What?" Olivia said, a yawning pit of apprehension opening in her stomach. "What do you mean? Who was it then?"

"That was Noah Pritchard himself."

"But, but ... I thought the great Noah Pritchard was a recluse and never appeared in public. What's he doing pretending to be a gallery owner?"

"To be fair. He didn't say he *was* the gallery owner. In fact, when he first appeared in the back before he found you that dustpan and brush, he was calling for the gallery owner. Didn't you hear him? He was calling for Rob. That would be Rob, the gallery owner."

But Olivia was too irate. "Fancy him masquerading as a gallery owner instead of saying who he was."

"What difference would that have made? I still broke his bauble."

"Well ... Um ..." Olivia started the engine, and they drove off, back to Baublesville, where she felt safe.

She was going to stay there forever and never leave her home town again!

"I'm just an unholy bauble-breaker," Mel whispered. "A bauble-breaker am I." She glanced at Olivia before dissolving into shrieks of nervously hysterical giggles.

Chapter 2

OLIVIA LAY AWAKE FOR a long time, knowing she'd feel awful the following day for not getting enough sleep. There was nothing she could do about it, though, because the words, "Your apologies won't restore what's been broken. Some things are beyond repair" kept playing on a loop in her head, keeping sleep away.

She knew all this mithering over historical events had been sparked by the bauble incident.

It had been this time of year, too, that she'd been going to marry Mike six years ago. They were in her living room, surrounded by wedding preparations, relishing all the details leading up to the big day.

When she'd heard the door creak, she

turned with a welcoming smile to see Mike holding a box in his hands. His tense expression and complete stillness warned Olivia that something was amiss.

"What is it?" she'd asked when he'd continued to stand there saying nothing, just staring at her with accusation in his eyes.

"Olivia, what's this?" he'd demanded, his voice hard. He held up the box in which she kept her most private things, including some old letters and mementos.

Her spirits plummeted as she recognised the old metal-bound mahogany box she'd kept hidden away for years. "What are you doing with that? That's mine. It's private."

He ignored her question. "You kept letters from him all this time? Letters from your pen pal, Thomas?"

Olivia took a deep breath, trying to find the right words. "Yes, Thomas was my childhood pen pal. We lost contact for years until we reconnected as adults and spent a while indulging in nostalgia for times gone by. That's all it was. But what do you think you're doing reading my private letters?"

Mike's face tightened even more. "Nostalgia? And you didn't think to tell me about it? We were supposed to be building a life together, Olivia. Keeping this from me feels like a betrayal and makes me wonder what else you're hiding."

"I'm so sorry, Mike. It wasn't about hiding anything from you. I didn't think it would be a big deal. I didn't think of it at all. However, I do object to you prying into my things."

He still ignored what she had to say. "Your apologies won't restore what's been broken. Some things are beyond repair," he'd retorted.

"Well, yes. Yes, they are," she'd said in return. "I have the right to my own private memories, even in a life we would have shared. And I have the right to have my own concerns heard, too. You're not even listening to them."

And that had been that. She couldn't believe it when it happened. All that happiness, all those promises for a wonderful future – all gone. Just like that.

She tossed around in her bed, searching for a comfortable spot, yet memories continued to flood in. She'd confided in Mel. Of course she had. She'd always confided in Mel.

"He was so hurt, Mel," she'd said. "I never meant to keep anything from him. I didn't even think of it."

Mel, as she always did, had listened attentively. "Olivia, you didn't do anything wrong. I can't believe he reacted that way over some old letters. He should have trusted you," she'd said. "I'm afraid some insecurities can't be appeased. And it sounds as if Mike has some extremely well-hidden insecurities. Also, what *was* he doing poking about in your stuff?"

"But I loved him, Mel," Olivia had replied. "And I thought he loved me, too."

Looking back over the years, she now wondered if either of those things had been true. Mel had realised at the time that they couldn't have been. She'd said, "Love is not enough if it's built on insecurity and mistrust. You deserve someone who can love you completely, without those kinds of doubts."

Olivia gave up trying to sleep and climbed out of bed.

In her sock drawer she found her old document box and spent a happy hour reading through those letters again. They never failed to bring back a carefree, idyllic childhood. She wondered what Thomas was doing these days and hoped he was happy wherever he was.

They'd never met, but they hadn't needed to for their period of letter-writing to have brought so much contentment to them both.

Olivia went back to bed and fell asleep wondering how on earth she was going to cope with the bill for three dozen way-too-expensive glass baubles.

It was better than worrying that there was no one who would ever love her completely, without any doubts.

Chapter 3

A WEEK LATER, MEL, with a sly glance Olivia's way, said, "I've been asking around …"

Olivia was deep into rearranging a shelf of snow globes. She took her display duties very seriously. As she polished each snow globe and arranged it carefully on the shelf, she also inspected it for flaws and just to take in the beauty of each one. Snow globes were one of her favourite items of stock.

"Mmm?" she said, realising Mel had said something. "Asking about what?"

"Noah Pritchard, of course," her friend said. "Our favourite snarky gallery-owner who isn't a gallery-owner."

"Might be *your* favourite snarky

gallery-owner," Olivia muttered. "Not mine. What's much more important is working out where we can display these thirty-six glass baubles we have on order. Where will they be safe from clumsy members of the public?"

"Ha! You're looking at me, aren't you?"

"Maybe." Olivia laughed.

Mel pretend-pouted and then brightened again. "But you're not going to change the subject. Our famous recluse ..."

"*Your* famous recluse," Olivia corrected her. "Yours."

"*Our* famous recluse was on the verge of a fantastic career, known worldwide for his incredible way with glass, and his unique creations. He was engaged to be married to a childhood friend – awww – imagine that – they'd always known since they met aged six – that they'd marry. Fern – such a lovely name."

She handed Olivia the next snow globe for inspection.

"Anyway," she went on. "They were about to get married. He'd been offered a major exhibition in Paris, so they were going to go there on honeymoon ..."

Despite herself, Olivia was interested now. "Well?" she prompted, as Mel hesitated. "What happened? Why aren't they married now? I take it they're not married now."

"No. They're not married now. Fern died."

"Oh! I wasn't expecting that."

"Neither were they. It was a very sudden cardiac death. No one knew she had this undiagnosed heart condition. It killed her the week before the marriage and the exhibition. So he didn't go through with either."

Olivia felt awful for the young couple she was hearing about. How tragic.

"Since then, by all accounts," Mel went on. "He's kept himself to himself and done nothing but work with his glass. He's only recently started to send it into the outer world, too, via an agent. It's highly sought after, as one might expect. I don't know what he was doing in the gallery yesterday. How unfortunate that the first time he goes out in public I should smash his pride and joy bauble."

Mel was trying to keep her voice even but Olivia knew she was blaming herself for ruining Noah's first venture out.

It couldn't be undone now, though. "Come on," she said bracingly. "Give me a hand clearing out these musical boxes – I think we'll use this space for the Noah Pritchard baubles – it's high enough up to prevent at least children from having any, uh, accidents."

"I'm going to ask him if he's got some heart-shaped baubles. People do love hearts in all their forms." Olivia was conscious of Mel peering slyly at her. She ignored her.

But she did feel obliged to say: "Even if he does, we can't afford them. His work is far too expensive to have in here. The baubles we've already got coming are never going to sell!"

"Ooh," Mel squeaked. "Talking of which, I think they're here." She gestured towards the window through which Olivia could see a tall figure parked outside delving into the boot and carefully removing a box, which he carried with great care towards the shop.

"I've just remembered I have to go and ..."

"No!" Mel shrieked. "You can't leave me alone with him. Also, you can't leave me alone with his baubles. As it were."

Reluctantly Olivia stayed where she was but she concentrated really hard on dusting the musical box she was about to move. She heard Mel opening the door to save Noah balancing the box while he tackled it. She could hear Mel's excited babble as it came closer and closer to where she was trying to squeeze herself into the depths of the shelf now.

She could always tell how thrilled Mel was with anything by how high her squeaks got. Just now they were indecipherable.

When the squeaking stopped, Olivia slowly backed away from the shelf and straightened up to see Noah Pritchard standing there, box in hand, gazing steadily at her.

Mel was, predictably, grinning all over her face.

The silence went on too long until he broke it. "Is that shelf for the baubles?" he asked. "Shall I put them out there. Will you be arranging them on a small tree or placing them in beds of fur or coils of tinsel or putting them all in a big bowl? How were you thinking of displaying them?"

"Because we don't want people coming along and smashing them to smithereens," Olivia said. "I considered display cases but they're not very user-friendly for the customer. We try to be user-friendly in here." Olivia knew she was waffling, but she couldn't seem to stop herself. "As it were," she added, suddenly realising by Mel's smirk that them being user-friendly might sound a bit ... a bit ... something or other.

Something that made Mel smirk, anyway. Smutty. That's what her friend could be. Just smutty.

"Yep. Nothing like someone smashing a bauble to make them feel right at home," Noah said, his face straight.

Mel shrieked with delight. She was obviously a fan already, but Olivia was made of sterner stuff and wasn't going to fall so easily for this obnoxious man who seemed to think he was somehow a cut above everyone else.

"I considered individual stands so they can hang safely and be admired without the need of touching," Olivia went on, determined to get through this with her dignity intact this time. "Obviously with focused and adjustable spotlights."

"Obviously," he agreed. "Can I put this box down now?"

"Of course," Mel squeaked. "Here." She patted the top shelf.

Olivia noticed the completely charming smile he sent Mel's way as he placed the box carefully where she'd indicated. She hoped he didn't send one like that her way.

She might fall for it.

She said: "I thought I could put small signs describing each bauble's unique features, and price, of course, providing interesting information on each piece."

"They're all packed in their own boxes inside the big box," he said. "So they come with their own packaging, too."

"He's thought of everything!" Mel squeaked. "Everything." She gazed up at him as if she'd found a new set of feet at which to worship.

Mel was starstruck. Completely smitten.

It made it more challenging for Olivia to play it cool. But she was going to make her best effort.

"Including the price," Olivia muttered to herself, nearly choking when she saw a tag. She had been unable to bring herself to look at the receipt and had merely shoved it into her accounts drawer when they'd got home last week.

"Pardon?" Noah said.

"Oh, nothing," Olivia wished she'd not said it aloud. It had been the shock. It had made her blurt out her thoughts. "It was very kind of you to deliver them yourself. I'm a bit surprised. I thought you were a recluse, and yet we saw you the other day at the gallery and now here you are again."

She was aghast that she'd actually said it. It must still be the shock of the price.

Into the small silence that fell she could clearly hear Mel gushing to customers who'd come into the shop: "... yes, and we have some genuine Noah Pritchard baubles this year. Not only that but we have *the* genuine Noah Pritchard here at the moment, too. Look. He's the tall, handsome man at the back of the shop where Olivia is keeping him to herself."

Olivia went hot. She went cold. She couldn't bring herself to look at Noah.

She decided she was going to kill her friend the first moment she got. She bared her teeth at Mel as her friend gambolled over to them like an oversized lamb. Mel actually winked at her, and merely beamed back. Then she bounced over to Noah and gazed adoringly up at him.

"Noah!" she said. "We could really do with some baubles that are heart-shaped. Heart-shaped items whizz off the shelf. Say you'll make some for us!" She waited breathlessly for his reply.

Olivia was amused to see him rear back like a startled cobra. "No! Way too schmaltzy! Commercial tat. My baubles are art, not sentimental bling. You will never catch me making anything heart-shaped!"

The horror on his face was almost laughable, but poor Mel. She looked like a trod-on puppy. Olivia leapt into the fray: "And we sell commercial tat. We don't want anything else in here that's likely to give our customers heart attacks when they see the price tag," she said. "So, good idea, Mel, but we don't want anything else from the great Noah Pritchard. Anything."

"You don't believe in investing in art?" Noah enquired.

Olivia said, "I believe in investing in things that won't leave me bankrupt. Anyway, we've done enough investing in *your* business already. I'm going to save the rest of my money for some lovely over-sentimental snowmen made of candy-floss and glitter, maybe some neon-coloured reindeer, maybe some lovely pink ribbon wreaths for the door. Anything that adds a touch of whimsy and charm to the season."

"Whimsy?" Noah said. "More like a saccharine overdose of holiday cheer. It's as if you've cranked up every Christmas cliché to levels never seen before."

"Maybe what we're investing in, is seasonal cheer; maybe we're investing in memories; maybe we're investing in making people happy. It doesn't have to have a heart-attack-high price tag to be an investment in the magic of Christmas. Try looking beyond the tinsel and find the joy in it all."

His face suddenly clouded as if she'd jabbed him in a sore spot and reminded him that he had no joy. He headed for the door saying over his shoulder, "I'm surprised you don't have a grotto complete with helper-elves and a fat Santa!"

"That's coming next week!" she retorted, conscious of Mel's start of surprise.

And, damn! Now she'd have to sort out

a grotto and a fat Santa. "Along with inflatable reindeer for the roof," she shouted after him, now maddened beyond reason.

Chapter 4

"We've sold another of Noah's baubles," Mel said, ringing up the till as if it was a personal victory.

"Hmphh!" was the only answer Olivia felt able to give, although she was so very relieved that she wasn't going to be stuck with her rash purchase of three dozen of them. They had cost such a lot of money she had been in danger of losing her business over them. And all because that man's pompous disdain got under her skin.

"How thoughtful of him to provide us with all the packaging materials for each bauble," Mel said. It was as if she couldn't get enough of praising Noah Pritchard.

"At that price he should have provided

velvet-lined boxes," Olivia mumbled. "Ouch!" She'd jabbed herself with the sharp end of an artificial holly pick.

"Serves you right, Grumpy!" Mel said while she looked for a plaster so Olivia's life blood didn't get all over the stock. "Are we ready with this afternoon's massive order?"

"Nearly. I just have to find a few more tatty baubles and a bit more tacky bling and there'll be more than enough stuff for the Baublesville Christmas tree."

"Don't be so ungracious. Noah didn't have to come here for the supplies, did he?"

"No." It would be ungracious of her to say anything else. But she always did feel ungracious when Noah Pritchard was the topic of conversation, and he seemed to always be the topic of conversation these days.

"Let me help," Mel said, coming round to where Olivia was packing the boxes with the supplies for the tree. "It was such a great idea of his to provide the village Christmas tree this year, and to decorate it himself as well. All for charity."

"You've become quite the fan," Olivia said dryly, carefully handing her friend another handful of holly picks.

"Well, he's broken out of recluse mode and it all seems to be so he can help others. What's not to like?" Mel queried.

"Has it got anything to do with Rob-the-gallery-owner turning up?"

Mel blushed. "It might have," she said. "You have realised it was him Noah was calling for when I broke that bauble, haven't you? So it was kind-of lucky I broke the bauble." She nudged Olivia as if she expected agreement.

"Fancy him turning out to be gallery-Rob. You know that's why Noah made some baubles in the first place, don't you – it was because Rob is his long-time friend, Fern's brother, and he asked him for some to help his gallery along a bit. Noah had only been persuaded to come down from his hillside retreat to the gallery be-cause Rob needed him there. What luck that was when we broke that bauble!"

"We? *We* didn't break that bauble. *You* broke that bauble!"

"What luck that was when *I* broke that bauble," she repeated, unabashed. "I couldn't have planned it better if I'd tried," Mel continued smugly, tucking in the final item, closing and taping shut the box.

"I'm not going to ask you what you mean by that, because I dread to think," Olivia said. "Anyway, it looks like our grotto has arrived." They both looked up to see a lorry parked outside the shop. Luckily, there was a covered area outside the back of the shop where they could erect their previously unexpected and un-planned for grotto.

"And, look, a lovely inflatable reindeer, too ..." Mel said. "For the roof," she added, as if Olivia didn't know what she was talking about.

Olivia cringed inside at the thought of the reindeer on the roof, but it was too late now. She had to go through with it. Thank heaven she hadn't said she'd have a Santa stuck in the chimney, too.

"How are you going to get it on the roof, Liv?" Mel enquired. She was grinning all over her face. "And when it's there, how much will it cost for Santa to park his sleigh and reindeer on your roof? Do tell."

"Pardon," Olivia said, completely at sea.

"Nothing is the answer," Mel chortled. "Nothing. Because it'll be on the house!"

It took a moment to sink in. "Arrghh!" Olivia groaned. "Have you been eating Christmas cracker jokes again?"

"Admit it – it sleighed you," Mel said, and ducked as if Olivia would throw something at her.

If only she had something to throw! Olivia looked around but there was nothing handy for the purpose.

"Better get to it," Mel said. "It looks like rein, deer."

"Gah!" Olivia clutched her head.

"And look, we have ladders," Mel added as Rob entered the shop, nodding his head to her.

"They're just outside," he said. "Lying underneath the window. I've got two," he said to Olivia, "so Mel and I can each hold one while you go up one and Noah goes up the other. I can't think how else you're going to get something that size on the roof."

"Noah?" Olivia queried. "It's his fault there's a socking great reindeer out there in the first place."

Rob looked puzzled so Mel kindly explained. "She only said she was having one for the shop because it was the tackiest thing she could think of after he'd said about all our stuff being tacky commercial tat. She always has to go one better, don't you, Livvy? Hence the reindeer with no eyes."

"It's got eyes," Rob said. "What are you talking about?"

"I have no eyed deer," Mel said entirely straight-faced.

Rob fell about laughing so hard he

couldn't breathe, much to Mel's huge delight.

Olivia had run out of groans. She rolled her eyes and went outside to check on the ladders. Yes, there were two where Rob had said there would be.

But, what about Noah? And was it going to be horribly awkward seeing him again?

She looked up at the roof. She wasn't that wildly keen on heights, but she'd have to go through with it now.

A voice interrupted her somewhat rueful thoughts. "Rob told me you needed help to get your, uh, charming reindeer on the roof. I don't know why he couldn't help you himself, but I decided to humour him by turning up anyway. I couldn't possibly miss this treat."

Olivia turned to see Noah smiling at her in such a way that she felt oddly shy.

"It's your fault we have to do this, anyway," she retorted, trying to cover up how weird she felt around him. "If you hadn't been going on about commercial tat, I wouldn't have insisted on getting more of it. You *made* me do it."

He laughed. It was a nice laugh. It sounded like home. Olivia felt even more awkward when she realised she was thinking such things.

"It's actually quite a nice looking reindeer," he said.

She looked at him suspiciously. The reindeer was awful. It had no redeeming features that she could see, except it came with its own integral platform to sit safely on the roof. It was a horrible yukky sandy brown, its antlers were crooked, and it had the most peculiar, leering expression on its face.

"Yes, it's lovely, isn't it," she agreed. "Just my cup of tea."

By now Mel and Rob had put up a ladder each and stood by the bottom waiting for Noah and Olivia to go up them with the reindeer.

"Oh, for the love of tinsel, you two. Get on with it!" Mel said.

"Ready, steady, ho-ho-go!" Rob shouted.

"Come on, let's get out of here. I can't stand it any longer. If we're really lucky we might get some peace on the roof," Olivia said, bending to pick up her end of Sandy the reindeer.

Noah bent to his end, too, and they simultaneously ascended their respective ladders carrying Sandy between them.

He was heavier than Olivia had expected but she hung on and put one foot on the next rung, followed by the other. Until it wobbled and threatened to take them down with it. "Eek!" she yelled. "Stop a minute til we get steady again. Hold on, Noah! We can't let Sandy defeat us!"

Noah said: "Sandy?"

"Yes, Sandy. Sandy the yuk reindeer," Olivia said. She'd steadied herself now and put her foot on the next rung again. "But we're okay. We have the expert glassblower and the commercial tatter here to save the day."

"Tatter?"

"Um. Well. Yes. Tatter." Was that even a word? she wondered. They'd made the roof by now, but Olivia hadn't considered what happened next. "Um. Now what?"

"Well, luckily, the expert glassblower has

brought the necessary items to anchor the platform to the roof." Noah grinned at her while dragging a bag Olivia hadn't previously noticed over his head and rootling about in it. "Teamwork makes the dream work, right?"

"Oh, no! You've caught the Christmas cracker bug the others have got. And I'm stuck on the roof with it. Oh, woe is me!"

"Yes, but it's all been worth it hasn't it. I mean, look at that majestic creature, standing tall, looking out over the village as if surveying his domain. I'm pretty sure it's the most impressive thing in the whole village."

She tried to say, "You're not wrong," and nearly choked. She tried again, "And I have you to thank for making it all happen."

"Well, I'm always here to save the day when it comes to inflatable reindeers. Especially ones that come with their own handy platform."

"I don't know how you kept your face straight when you said that," Olivia said. "It's got to be the tackiest item you've ever touched in your whole life."

He turned to her with a grin. Goodness! Was that the first grin she'd seen on his face? It was so infectious, she felt her own face creasing around her answering one. But before she could say anything, Mel's voice came floating up to them: "Well, well, well, what do we have here? A couple of merry elves perched atop the roof with Rudolph?"

"It's not Rudolph, it's Sandy!" Olivia and Noah said in unison, laughing.

Until they heard the sound of ladders falling on the ground.

"What are you doing with the ladders?"

Mel said, "Ladders? What ladders? We don't see any ladders."

"You two look good up there, like a pair of vintage Christmas ornaments," Rob said.

"Vintage?" Noah queried.

Olivia sat down with a bump when she realised what Mel and Rob had done. "Hey!" she yelled. "What if we fall off? What then?" But all she heard in reply was muffled giggles. Idiots!

She felt a hand on her arm and looked up.

Noah said: "I won't let you fall off."

"Oh." She didn't know what to say. "Trouble is," she said. "If I do fall off and you try to stop me, it might mean you fall off with me."

"Oh, well. We'll either stay on the roof together or we'll fall off together."

She was content with that and allowed herself to lean on him as they sat together on the little platform which, thankfully, was now stable.

Olivia didn't lean her full weight on him, though. This camaraderie was too new to trust.

She had never been on the roof of Baubles and Bling before. It was an experience she would not have missed for all the tinsel on the tree.

Darkness closed in and tranquillity enveloped her. A tapestry of stars appeared across the sky while the moon cast a silvery sheen over the countryside blanketing the world with serenity. Christmas lights in the village twinkled. She could hear snatches of carol singing and laughter, smell the scent of pine on the wintry air mingling with the smoky aroma from someone's chimney.

The air was cold, but it was as if she was leaning back on her own hot water bottle and the heat spread out from that contact with Noah and kept her warm.

There was such stillness, such peace, that Olivia felt herself succumbing to the enchantment of it all, the magic of the night and the season. Looking across the countryside, she could see the outline of distant hills and the dark silhouettes of trees, their branches frosted with a delicate layer of snow.

She knew that whatever might happen after tonight, this moment would always hold a place in her most cherished memories.

They were in a world of their own, untouchable. Maybe she wouldn't yell at Mel and Rob for running off with the ladders, after all.

"You know, I've always loved Christmas. It reminds me of the joy and warmth of my childhood. My parents turned our house into a magical wonderland every year. Looking back, it all seemed so idyllic. No worries. The decorations, the carols, the smell of hot chocolate and gingerbread, spending time with my parents – it all brings back happy memories. Every item I handle in my shop brings back the joy of that time. There's nothing like it."

"I used to love Christmas too. But after I lost Fern, it merely served to become a painful reminder of my loss. I have been avoiding it ever since. I am beginning to realise now that, although it was my instinct to withdraw from life in every way, it can't have been very helpful for Rob, or for his mother."

"Everyone grieves differently," Olivia said. She was reluctant to say more in case she said the wrong thing. She hoped her silent company might bring some small comfort.

Mel and Rob didn't leave them there too long. They brought the ladders back, Olivia and Noah safely descended to ground level again whereupon much mulled wine and many mince pies were consumed in Baubles and Bling to celebrate the arrival of Sandy on the roof and seasonal goodwill all round.

Chapter 5

IT WAS ONLY THROUGH Mel, who was Olivia's personal news source of everything local, that she discovered Noah had volunteered to provide a very large Christmas tree for the village square.

He was not only providing the tree but he was going to decorate it, too, which would be a massive undertaking given how enormous the tree was.

Olivia had seen it in place a couple of days ago. Mel had told her Noah was down there now starting to adorn the boughs.

He'd had a fence erected all around while he worked on it. Olivia wondered if that was so he didn't have to talk to anyone because he was so unsociable, or whether it was because he needed peace whenever he was creating any-thing.

Both reasons made her hesitate but, spurred on by Mel's encouragement that Noah's la-di-da over-the-top artistic pretensions needed to be kept in check, she had decided to make herself approach him and offer to help, even if all she did was hold things and pass them at his command.

Outside the fence, a crowd of people circulated with mulled cider and gingerbread. Olivia stopped to get a tray of supplies. It was all to raise funds for good causes so she was happy to load up with way too many edible goodies.

Carols rang out into the wintry evening. She felt almost tearful. Everything about it was so beautiful, so nostalgic and lovely.

There were baskets for people to drop off gifts of all kinds to be distributed to those who might otherwise have too threadbare a Christmas. At the end of the festivities there would be an auction for one of Noah's pieces of work, too.

She carried the tray to where Noah was

working. As she got nearer she saw him impatiently remove a decoration he'd already placed in order to carefully put it elsewhere. Crikey. They'd never be done if he was going to keep that up!

Olivia put the tray down on a box and picked up one of Noah's baubles. She chose her spot and carefully made sure its ribbon was well on the branch she'd chosen before standing back to admire it: "Ah, there we go, a touch of elegance amidst the, uh, festive chaos."

He started as if he'd been in a world of his own and let out a little laugh. "Festive chaos? Those decorations, which I obtained from the renowned Christmas emporium in the village, known as 'Baubles and Bling', represent the joy and spirit of Christmas, Ms Olivia, I'll have you know."

She smiled. He was getting it!

"I'm pleased to say that mixing your wonderful glass baubles with my, uh glitter and glitz adds a unique charm to the tree."

"You are so right. This tree would be nothing without your baubles and bling. Nothing!"

"Exactly!" Olivia agreed. "The Baublesville Christmas tree – a blend of elegance and whimsy."

Olivia couldn't remember the last time she'd smiled so much, and every time she tried not to smile so much, it kept breaking out again.

This Christmas, out of all Christmases, was proving to be more magical than she could ever have imagined.

Chapter 6

"Well, I think it looks stunning," Olivia said, standing back to admire their joint creation. "Let's go for a hot chocolate to celebrate. And to dilute all this mulled cider."

"Good idea! Then I'll swing by afterwards just to make sure everything's stayed in the right place."

"Does that mean you'll be swinging by on a regular basis to move things by a centimetre or two?" Olivia was laughing, but she'd seen him agonize over the tiniest placements and change things around because the colour combinations didn't look right to him."

"I might," he said, looking suddenly shy.

Seated at an outside table so they could

enjoy the view, Noah and Olivia remained in companionable silence for a while until Olivia couldn't help herself and said it again: "I think it looks stunning! I do!"

Noah said, "It's the mix of art and tat that does it – the combination of style and whimsy. It's a great mix."

She'd never seen him look so relaxed. She was marvelling over it as she watched his face. He said, "It was fun to do. If not for you I would never have thought to do it. Thank you. And ... Oh ..."

Olivia glanced behind her where Noah was looking. An older woman approached. Olivia turned back to Noah. He looked appre-hensive.

"What's wrong?" she whispered.

Noah, his voice low, said: "It's Fern and Rob's mother. She's never got over the loss of her daughter. She feels no one else should get over it, either. It's hardest on Rob, but spreads to me, too. I'm never sure how to deal with it."

"Oh, dear," Olivia said. "That sounds difficult. I wonder how come she's here." She stopped talking as Fern's mother was almost on them.

"Noah, is that you?" the new arrival said. "It's been so long!"

"Yes, it's been a while. I hope you're well, Brenda," he said. "Let me introduce you to …"

But the older woman interrupted him. "I heard you were spending a lot of time in Baublesville," she said, glaring accusingly at Olivia who smiled feebly at her. Brenda looked back at Noah. "You seem to have come out of your shell, Noah." She didn't sound as pleased as Olivia thought she should.

But then, she'd never lost a daughter so how would she know how Brenda was supposed to sound.

Even so, it seemed a bit mean to take it out on Noah all these years later. Olivia was horribly afraid looking at Noah that the progress he'd made in recent weeks was lost. His face once again wore that guarded, supercilious look that had so put her back up when she'd first met him in the gallery.

She was horrified at the feeling of loss it gave her to see the Noah she'd been getting to know vanish in front of her eyes.

"I see you've lost all your artistic ambitions, too," Brenda went on to say. "Commercial baubles. Really, Noah? That's not exactly your style is it. Fern had such good taste, too. How could you besmirch her memory like this?" She even turned slightly to look Olivia up and down like she was a side of meat.

Brenda didn't have to say anything. There might as well have been a neon arrow above her head pointing to the tasteless member of their company who was, no doubt, the one corrupting the peerless Noah Pritchard.

Olivia felt as if the Noah of recent days was melting away.

A new voice joined in. Rob had arrived. He didn't hesitate. He waded right in: "Mum! Noah is his own person, and he deserves happiness. Leave him alone." He turned to Olivia and muttered: "I'm so sorry, Liv."

She could do nothing but shake her head at him. She didn't dare speak.

"This is none of your business, Rob," his mother said.

"Of course it is! Fern is my sister. She wouldn't agree with the way you are, either. And she definitely wouldn't agree with you treating Noah so unfairly. You can't force him to live in the past forever."

Noah put his hand on Rob's shoulder. "Thank you, Rob. But it's all right. I need to deal with this in my own way."

He could barely bring himself to look at her, so Olivia stepped back, hoping to fade into the shadows.

It was apparent Rob didn't want to back down, but the expression on Noah's face was so grim that he did, saying: "All right, Bro, but you know we've got your back." He gestured at Olivia to include her, and she was grateful for that even though Noah still didn't look at her.

Although she now knew Noah used that haughty façade to hide grief and pain, she hated to see it and was afraid he was withdrawing too deep to ever surface again.

An inner freezing chill threatened to over-whelm her. She had to keep her face straight. She had to get away without breaking down. The loss she felt was unbearable.

Olivia said, "I'd better leave you all to catch up."

Brenda immediately said, "Yes, thank you. Good idea."

Olivia pretended not to see the hand Noah immediately held out as if to stop her going. She was so afraid of collapsing in a sobbing heap.

She was also afraid of intruding on such an old and close family relationship.

Chapter 7

the unexpected skirmish to her later. "Rob's told
me about his mother. She appears determined to
grieve for Fern forever, and expects everyone else
to do the same."

She sighed noisily. "She's even tried to stop
Rob from moving on from the loss of his sister,
too. Brenda resents anyone's joy, but especially
those who knew Fern. I know it stems from her
grief, but it's really not fair on anyone else."

Mel pouted and Olivia wondered if Brenda was going to put a spoke in the wheel of that
budding romance, too. That would be awful.
Rob and Mel got on so well together and Olivia
had never seen her friend so happy.

She checked out Mel's face again and thought maybe Brenda had already had a dampening effect in that quarter.

"Brenda is bound to be in pain," she said slowly. "She must have had such a strong bond with Fern."

"Rob has tried to talk to her. But how often can the same words be said? That moving on doesn't mean forgetting, that it's not a betrayal of her memory, but rather a way to honour her by embracing life and joy. Fern would have wanted that."

Mel shrugged, "But the last time he tried to talk to her she got really mad and said how would he know what Fern would have wanted? Trouble is, he misses Fern, too, so all this is hard for him as well. But he knows that Fern would hate this."

She kept polishing the shelf as if it was trying to stop her. "We can keep her memory alive without it ruining our present lives," She added sadly. "And it's a bit of a double whammy because he's been so chuffed to see Noah coming to life again and now Brenda's going to try and ruin it."

"I feel so helpless," Olivia said. "I don't know either Noah or Brenda well enough to say anything. I never even knew Fern. It feels like it's not my business."

"Except it is your business if it's going to stop Noah and you getting together."

"Maybe we weren't meant to be. I mean, what with him being a well-thought of serious artist and me just being someone who sells tat. We're worlds apart," Olivia said.

She slumped in her seat. She should have known it was too good to be true. She should have known that no one could love her enough to get past their own demons. Mike had taught her that.

"Don't be daft!" Mel said, but she took another look at Olivia's face and appeared to decide that discretion was the better part of valour and changed the subject. "Rob and I are going to put a bauble on the Memorial Tree for Fern."

"Oh, my goodness. I haven't been to the

Memorial Tree this festive season yet. Has it been put up in the usual place?"

"Yes. On that little green space near the duck pond where everyone goes to sing carols. It always looks so lovely. Will you be going with your baubles for your mum and dad? Like you usually do. Can I come with you? Like I usually do."

"Of course. It wouldn't be the same without you. I must confess I snaffled a couple of the baubles I liked best when Noah's were delivered. They are a bit expensive for me, but they are so beautiful, I couldn't resist, and I know Mum and Dad will love them."

"Ha! I noticed there were only thirty-four on the shelves. That's where they went. Anyway, I don't think I've told you but that whole thing about Noah making any baubles at all – I found out how that came about from Rob. I mean, it was odd that the great Noah Pritchard should make something as tacky as Christmas baubles."

Olivia knew that Mel was trying to distract her from dwelling on the ruins of her emerging love affair with Noah.

As she thought it, for the first time she accepted that was what it was – she'd been falling in love with him. Oh, how she hoped it hadn't gone so far that it was going to be hell losing it before she'd properly gained it.

"Okay. Tell me the story of how the great Noah Pritchard lowered himself enough to create tacky baubles. I'm all ears."

Mel gave her a sharp look but continued with her story. "He made one for Fern. Rob saw it when he visited Noah. There it was, hanging from its own little stand. It was, or I should say, it 'is', tear-shaped, and the most beautiful thing Rob had ever seen. He asked Noah what he was going to do with it and got no answer. Maybe there wasn't an answer."

Mel stopped for a moment and looked around the shop as if just realising where she was. She gave Olivia a quick smile and carried on: "Rob told Noah it would be perfect for the Memorial Tree this Christmas season, whereupon Noah's face took on that terrified-don't-make-me-go-out-in-public look he has, so Rob asked him if he could do it for him."

Olivia was imagining a studio full of beautiful pieces with Rob and Noah studying the most exquisite artwork of all in there; trying to decide how to deal with it.

"I think Noah was reluctant for the bauble to go out in public as if it was a part of himself, but in the end, when Rob said it would be good for Brenda to see it and know that Fern hadn't ever been forgotten, he agreed."

Olivia knew she'd be unable to put her own ornaments on the memorial tree for her mum and dad without finding the tear-shaped one for Fern, too. She had a strong feeling she needed to see it to fully know Noah. She wanted to see all his work. She wanted to know him.

Mel spoke and Olivia jumped in surprise. She tried to look as if she'd been listening intently as her friend carried on. "So Rob asked Noah to make him one, too, for Fern. It was a long time after that he realised how great it would be to have Noah make some for his gallery – what a great selling point that would be – real artistic Noah Pritchard baubles."

Mel stopped to sell a customer some holly picks and a packet of dark blue and silver tinsel. "So, where was I? Oh, yes, that took a lot more arm-twisting but, in the end, Noah agreed when Rob said it would help him make ends meet in the gallery. Funny how it all fits together," she said, a dreamy look on her face.

Olivia wasn't sure if the dreaminess was for the way the story of the Fern-baubles ran along so well, or whether it was the thought of how she and Rob fit together.

And she wasn't going to ask.

Chapter 8

THERE FOLLOWED FIVE DAYS of awful, waiting anxiety.

Five days of no Noah. Five days of no Rob. Nothing.

"Not that we have any right to expect anything," Olivia said, taking another gulp of mulled wine from one of the really, really tacky mulled wine glasses she stocked in the shop.

They had reindeer prancing all around them. Of course they did. Probably all those reindeer were called Sandy. Or Comet or Dasher or something. Sandy was best, though. Would always be the best name for a reindeer.

"I mean, who are we to expect anything from anyone? We're just us. We're not anyone in particular. We can't compete with the past."

Mel snatched up the bottle and put the top on it. "I think you've had quite enough of that alcohol, young lady," She said. "It's bed for you now. Off you go. I'll close up."

They were very busy in the shop. It was the only thing that stopped them drinking too much mulled wine and getting too maudlin every night.

Olivia had never felt so disappointed, so sad. She felt like an interloper in a love story that had never, and would never, be hers. It would always only ever have the expected tragic ending. She would never have been enough to fill the void left by Fern.

She didn't deserve to be fully loved by any-one. Mike taught her that. It was silly of her to temporarily forget the lesson she'd learned back then.

Noah needed someone better than her to mend him. She ached for him and his grief, but he needed someone more suitable to deal with his loss, someone Brenda would accept for him.

In this realisation she acknowledged that she did love Noah, and she wanted to do whatever was right by him, but she also needed to work out what was best for her.

Should she pursue a love that may always be stunted by the past, or should she step back and allow herself and Noah the space they needed to heal?

Chapter 9

AND THEN, JUST AS suddenly, it all changed again.

Mel came into the shop that morning, bubbling over in Mel-fashion.

Without her saying a word, Olivia knew Rob was back in her life.

"We went to the tree," she said barely in the shop, still taking her coat off. "The Memorial Tree. We – that is Rob and me, in case you hadn't realised ..."

Olivia *had* realised. Who could have missed it!

"Rob and me, we took Brenda to the Memorial Tree to hang the bauble Rob had got Noah to make him for Fern, and so that Brenda could hang her Fern-memento, too. And we showed her the tear-shaped one that Noah had made all that time ago. It was so weird ..."

Mel broke off and her face took on a far-away look as if she relived the scene.

"Brenda – she stared at it for ages and kept asking us if Noah had really, really made it. We kept saying yes. I mean, who else could have made such an amazingly beautiful delicate thing, anyway? Finally, she stopped asking us and she just stared at it for so long we were afraid something horrible was happening to her."

Mel shook her head. "We didn't know what to do. We each took an arm in case she was going to collapse or something when suddenly she burst into tears and fell on Rob.

Just as well we'd been waiting for something to happen or he'd have gone down under the weight."

"It's not funny!" Olivia said, visualising the whole scene.

"No, I know. I'm trying not to cry myself telling you about it. It was as if the last seven years of grief poured out of her all at once."

Surreptitiously, Mel swiped at her eyes. "And then, the most peculiar thing. As if she suddenly realised she had to keep the bitterness going she straightened up away from Rob and snapped: "Ah, but – he's only made it now because he's got a guilty conscience since I saw him with *her*. That commercial tat woman.""

"I'm the commercial tat woman, I suppose," Olivia said. "Of course I am."

"Of course you are! All the commercial tat we both love so much – *that* commercial tat woman. What would we do without your ability to track down the most awful commercial tat? We'd be lost without all that magic you bring to the season. As you well know. Stop looking for compliments!

"I'm not!"

"Ha! Anyway, where was I? oh, yes – she'd suddenly thought of a reason not to trust Noah's intentions. She just wasn't prepared to let him off that easily."

"And?" Olivia knew something was coming, but she had no idea what it could be.

"And, as it turns out, Noah dates all his work, even the commercial tat."

"He does? I've never seen anything that looks like a date on the baubles."

"No, nor me. But when you know what to look for, there it is. So you can imagine the scene with villagers hanging their ornaments and tags on the Memorial Tree, remembering their loved ones; carol singers in attendance, and there's Rob and I using the lights on our mobile phones so she could peer at this bauble. She was so intent on finding the date I was terrified she would drop it and break it. All to prove Noah only made it out of a guilty conscience over the commercial tat woman."

"Well? Did she find it? The date?"

"Yes, she did. And Brenda was totally gob-smacked then because, of course, he'd made it months ago before any of this, before the Christmas season started."

"And before he met the commercial tat woman," Olivia said.

"That's right. Before he met you. Anyway, she insisted on taking down the bauble Rob had put up for his sister and checking the date on that, too. When she saw that was a date from months ago, as well, it was piteous, Livvy, piteous the way she seemed to collapse inside."

"It made her realise that she hadn't ever been alone in her grief, I suppose," Olivia whispered.

"I suppose so. She couldn't stop apologising to Rob for being so mean to him all this time when he's been grieving, too. And her whole face crumpled when she said how awful she'd been to Noah. Rob tried to tell her that they'd understood, but she was devastated that she'd tried to stand in the way of their happiness."

"That poor woman. Is she all right now?"

"Oh, yes. I mean, she feels terrible about Noah, and I don't know what she might do to make amends with him. But we took her to the café and forced hot chocolate and gingerbread on her, and lots of cuddles, and then took her home."

Mel couldn't help the little sniffle that accompanied her explanation. "Afterwards, Rob said he hadn't seen Brenda look that relaxed since before Fern died, so something has shifted. For the good. Maybe she can allow joy back into her own life now, too."

She looked bashful for a moment before adding, "And, I've never seen Rob look so relaxed either. It had a very good effect on him." She lowered her eyelashes and stared at the floor, but Olivia could clearly see the big grin under all the hair falling over her face.

Olivia laughed and pounced on Mel, giving her a big hug.

She couldn't help but sigh to herself when she thought back to the hurt on Noah's face after Brenda had confronted him, and the way he'd so obviously withdrawn from life again.

And the dreadful lost feeling it had given her. And still gave her.

But Noah came for her that night.

As soon as she saw him, she knew he and Brenda had made peace.

She was happy for him. But she was also on guard. Self-respect meant she couldn't allow anyone to pick her up when they felt like it, and then dump her when they felt like it, only to pick her up again when they felt like it. No matter how sympathetic she might have been for his state of mind.

"Come with me," he said. "Come with me to the Baublesville Christmas tree."

"What's at the tree? Carol singing?" She wondered at his eagerness. "Are we putting more stuff on the tree?"

She was desperate to ask him how he was after seeing Brenda, but if he didn't want to voluntarily tell her, she was damned if she was going to.

Did absolutely everything have to be

dragged out of him?

"Come on," he said, grabbing her hand and pulling her along. "Come on! I need you to see this."

They were at the Christmas tree now. Puzzled, she followed him around to the less public side of it. He pointed at a spot only he could see, and said, "There it is!"

"There what is?" She demanded looking at a load of fir boughs, and a bunch of tree ornaments, all beautiful but really what she could see in her own shop every day. "What? What is it?"

"Look more closely," he instructed as Olivia, completely confused, poked around in the darkness, carefully touching ornaments to keep them still so she could look at them properly, trying to find out what he meant, trying to find out what was going on.

She glanced at him and was struck by the look on his face. It was at once tender and apprehensive. What was going on?

"Go on, it's just there," he prompted, unable to contain himself any longer, pointing directly at the most exquisite thing she had ever seen.

It was a glass heart. A beautiful glass heart. Exactly the kind of thing Noah had sworn he'd never make because it was the epitome of commercial tat.

"Ha! Very funny!" she said, flicking it with her nail. It pinged with a lovely, clear crystal sound. "Where did you get this, then? It's not from my shop. Have you been buying stuff from other people's shops?"

He looked so horrified, that she flicked it again. This time she paid more attention to it. It produced a bright, clear sound with a beautiful resonance, a lovely, captivating musical note which seemed to accentuate the artistry and craftsmanship that had gone into creating such a delicate piece.

She turned to Noah, wondering at his silence. She saw he looked entirely serious. Doubt gripped her. What was going on?

"I made it," he said. "I made it in my studio this morning. It has today's date on it. It's, well, it's my heart. I made it for you. I want you to have it."

Olivia drew back and stared at him. He really did look as if he meant it. Did he really mean it? Could it be true? Tears started to her eyes and she tried to speak but only a croak came out.

"Was I mistaken?" he asked as the silence drew out. "When I practiced this it didn't sound nearly as schmaltzy as it does now, but maybe I needed to make it even *more* schmaltzy. Do you want more schmaltz? Should I have put a ribbon on it? I should have put a ribbon on it, shouldn't I?"

He looked so downcast she nearly laughed.

"I couldn't bring myself to put one of those embossed and die-cut tin hanger collar things on it which is what is usually used. I used gold instead. But I should have put a ribbon on it, shouldn't I? It should be more schmaltzy."

He seemed entirely sincere. Olivia tried hard to remember her own command to herself such a short while ago – to be self-respectful, to not allow anyone to pick her up when they felt like it, and then dump her when they felt like it, only to pick her up again when they felt like it.

But, hey – this was Noah Pritchard. *The* Noah Pritchard. *Her* Noah Pritchard.

"Yes, please," she whispered. "More schmaltz. More. More pink and fluffy. More romance. More heart stuff." She moved forward and his arms opened to enclose her as if they'd been waiting a long time for this very purpose.

"It's the only heart-shaped bauble I will *ever* make," he said. She could feel the words vibrating through this chest. "The only one. And it's yours."

"I will make sure to be very careful with it," she said. "I will treasure it. As I expect you to treasure mine, which you already have, schmaltzy though it might be," she said into his neck knowing that Christmas would be even more special than it had ever been before.

"Heartfelt Christmas to you, my schmaltzy, heart-blowing sweetheart."

The End

About the Author & Thank You

incredibly valuable for helping me reach a wider audience, (thus making sure I can keep writing books) (and PupperJack keeps getting his bones and gravy).

'Sweet Child of Yours' – A Smalltrees Series Book 1 – will be out by end June 2024

'Paws for Friends' – The Towering Trees Series Book 2 – will be out by end July 2024

A Christmas in Baublesville Sweet Romance 3 – will be out by end August 2024.

About the Author

Honey Stone is Susan Alison writing sweet romance – she lives in Bristol, UK, and writes and paints full-time. She paints dogs, especially Border Collies, Corgis, Whippets and Greyhounds. Every now and then she paints something that is *not* a dog just to show she's not completely under the paw – mainly, she's under the paw ...

Susan's romantic slice-of-life comedies, colouring books (traditional line art, and greyscale), illustrated doggerel, short stories can be found on Amazon. Writing as Honey Stone, her sweet romances are there, too. Pupper Jack has his own page, as well, for colouring books.

In the past, she was presented with the Katie Fforde Bursary Award for fiction (and she's still very chuffed about that!)

She can be contacted via her website at www.SusanAlison.combut, also, feel free to email SusanAlisonBooks@gmail.com if you'd like to receive her occasional newsletter.

Also By

Also published by Michael Villa Press:

Romantic Comedies by Susan Alison

Sweet romances by Susan Alison writing as

Honey Stone

Illustrated Short Stories in Large Print by Susan

Alison

Colouring books by Pupper Jack

see:

website: www.SusanAlison.com for

newsletter

sign-up on every page